This Ladybird book belongs to

. . . .

For Rosie
K.H.

LADYBIRD BOOKS
Ladybird Books is part of the Penguin Random House group of companies
whose addresses can be found at global.penguinrandomhouse.com.
www.penguin.co.uk   www.puffin.co.uk   www.ladybird.co.uk

Penguin
Random House
UK

First published 2023
001
Text and illustrations copyright © Kim Hillyard, 2023
The moral right of the author/illustrator has been asserted

Printed in China

The authorized representative in the EEA is Penguin Random House Ireland,
Morrison Chambers, 32 Nassau Street, Dublin D02 YH68

A CIP catalogue record for this book is available from the British Library

ISBN: 978–0–241–48860–7
All correspondence to:
Ladybird Books, Penguin Random House Children's
One Embassy Gardens, 8 Viaduct Gardens, London SW11 7BW

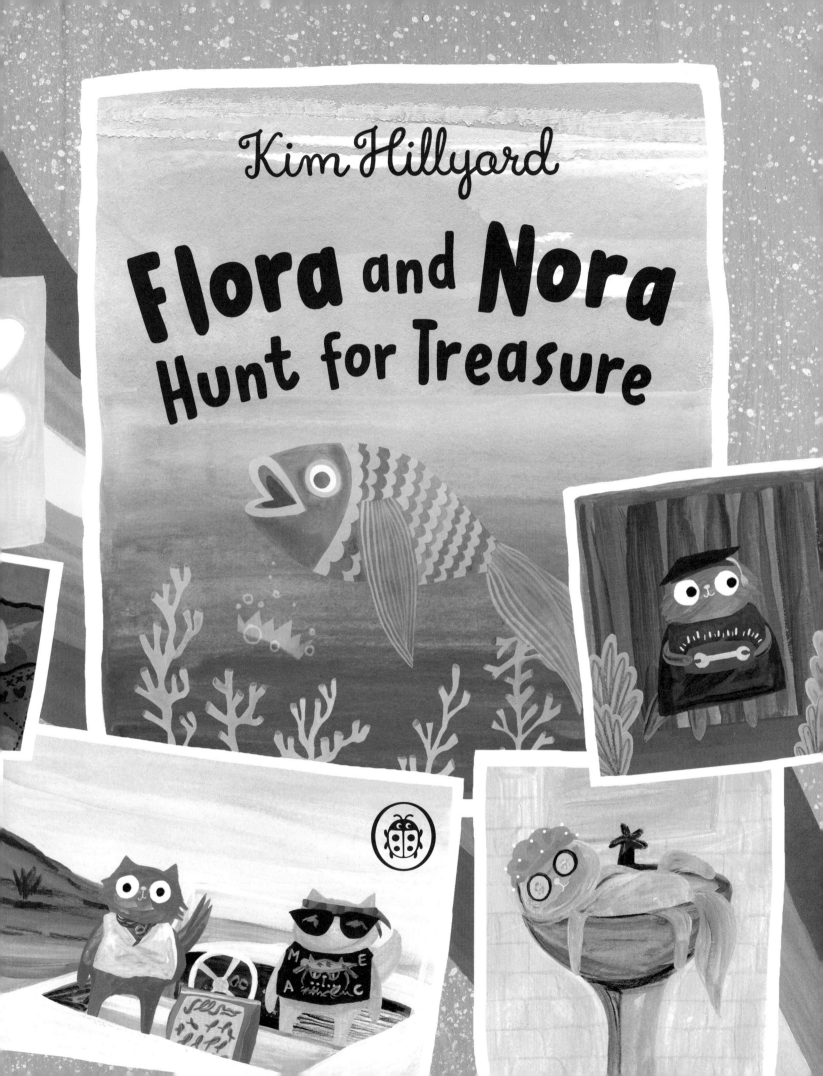

Flora is a cat with BRILLIANT ideas.

Nora is a cat with an ORGANIZED toolbox.

This is their ship.

Together, they sail through sunshine . . .

and rain,

easy times . . .

and hard times.

Everything is going swimmingly, when suddenly . . .

LIGHTNING STRIKES! (TWICE!)

Their ship splits in two!

Flora goes this way.

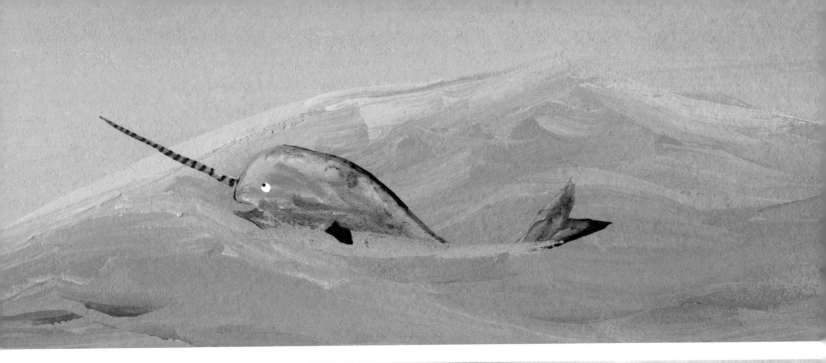

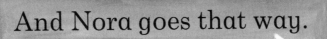

And Nora goes that way.

Soon, they are far away from each other!

Flora starts to panic.

Nora starts to cry.

But then they remember that friends do not always need
to be near each other for the magic of friendship to work.

So, when Flora gets sucked into a whirlpool, she thinks . . .

And when Nora gets trapped in the jaws of a very unreasonable sea serpent, she thinks . . .

WHAT WOULD FLORA DO?

Soon, they are back on track
to find each other and to find

THE SECRET TREASURE!

They sail alone
through tangled
trees . . .

soupy swamps . . .

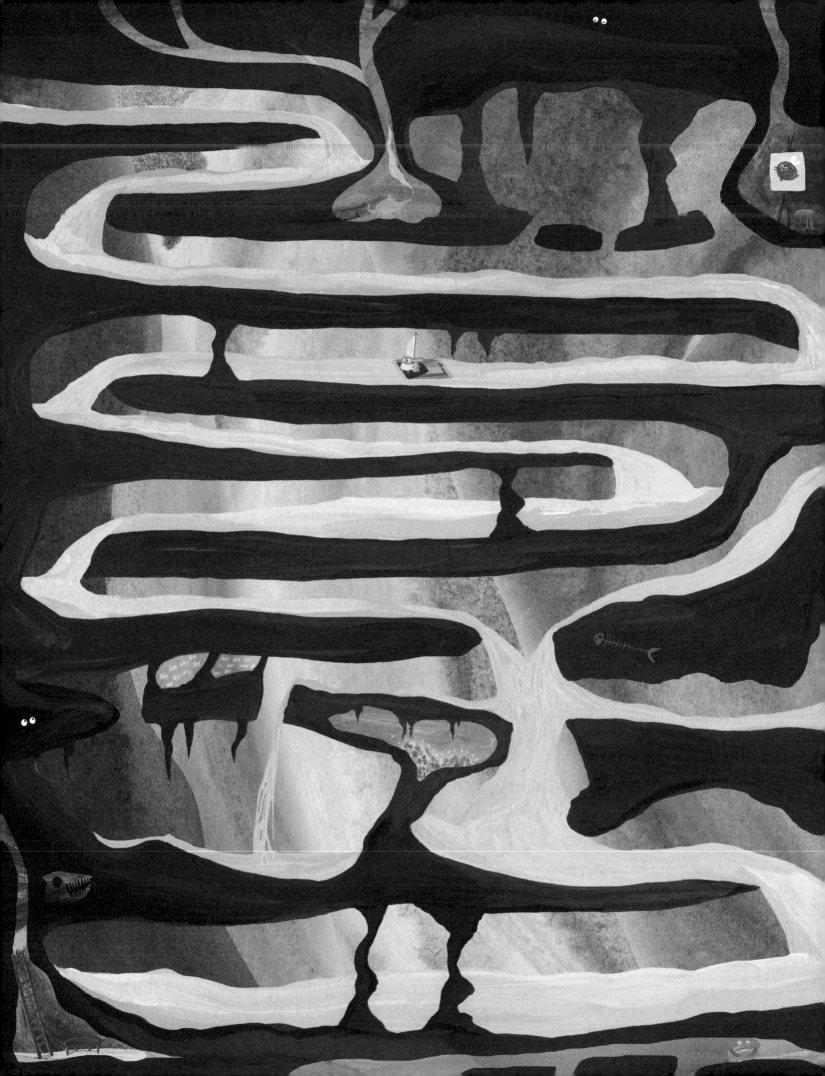

. . . and into caves that
seem to have
no end.

Finally, they both reach . . .

DRY LAND!
(WOOHOO!)

Flora runs this way.

Nora runs that way.

And soon, they are standing together beneath

THE
SECRET TREASURE!

THE SECRET TREASURE

* GLISTENS AND GLIMMERS
AND GLOWS!

But Flora is too busy hugging Nora to notice.

THE SECRET TREASURE

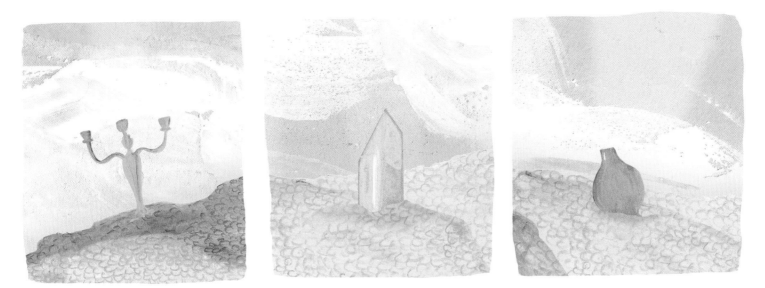

SPARKLES AND SHIMMERS AND SHINES!

But Nora is too busy admiring Flora's fancy new hat to see.

"I want you to have the treasure, Nora," says Flora.
"No, you take it, Flora," says Nora.

The two friends sit together in silence,
and then slowly start to smile.

"I've still got my organized toolbox," says Nora.
"And I've just had a brilliant idea!" says Flora.

So with a push and a shove . . .

a knock and a fix . . .

a lick of fresh paint . . .

and a
WHOLE LOT OF <u>LOVE</u>...

...they have a

NEW SHIP!

Flora and Nora wave goodbye to the island and the secret treasure, then sail away into the sunset.

Bright-blue waves carry them home.

And as they do, Flora and Nora
share stories of sea serpents and whirlpools,
and sing songs about having a friend by your side.

Which is the greatest
treasure of all.